From the Library of:

_____

_____

For my best friends—Bustopher, Gloria, and Perry

Copyright © 2020 by Stephanie Graegin

All rights reserved. Published in the United States by Schwartz & Wade Books, an imprint of Random House Children's Books, a division of Penguin Random House LLC, New York.

Schwartz & Wade Books and the colophon are trademarks of Penguin Random House LLC.

Visit us on the Web! rhcbooks.com
Educators and librarians, for a variety of teaching tools, visit us at RHTeachersLibrarians.com

Library of Congress Cataloging-in-Publication Data
Names: Graegin, Stephanie, author, illustrator.
Title: Fern and Otto: a story about two best friends / Stephanie Graegin.
Description: First edition. | New York: Schwartz & Wade Books, [2020] | Audience: Ages 3–7.
Summary: Best friends Fern the bear and Otto the cat meet various nursery rhyme and fairy tale characters on a walk through the forest to gather story ideas.
Identifiers: LCCN 2019042559 | ISBN 978-0-593-12130-6 (hardcover) | ISBN 978-0-593-12131-3 (library binding) | ISBN 978-0-593-12132-0 (ebook)
Subjects: CYAC: Best friends—Fiction. | Friendship—Fiction. | Authorship—Fiction. | Characters in literature—Fiction. | Bears—Fiction. | Cats—Fiction.
Classification: LCC PZ7.1.B4434 Fe 2020 | DDC [E]—dc23

The text of this book is set in Mrs. Eaves and Providence Sans Pro and hand-lettered.
The illustrations were rendered in pencil and assembled and colored digitally.
Book design by Stephanie Graegin, Rachael Cole, and Luke Wohlgemuth

MANUFACTURED IN CHINA
2 4 6 8 10 9 7 5 3 1
First Edition

FERN and OTTO

A Story About Two Best Friends

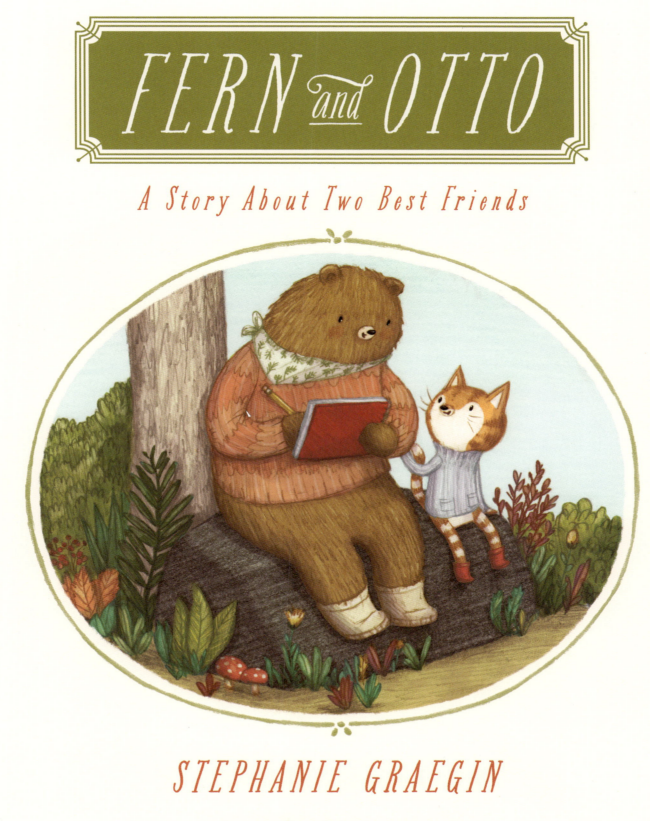

STEPHANIE GRAEGIN

schwartz & wade books · new york

Look who we have here! It's Fern and little Otto.
Fern is working on a story.
Otto is watching and trying to be helpful.
Shall we see what Fern has so far?

Fern and Otto are best friends.
They live in a cozy house on a hill, by the water.

They share tuna on toast for lunch
while listening to their favorite songs.

Afterward, they take catnaps in the sun.

A gentle breeze blows in through the window.

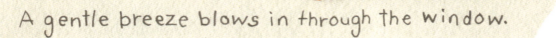

Fern? I love napping, but I don't want a story about it. Can't you make something exciting happen?

Fern reminds Otto of everything they enjoy doing together. But Otto just shakes his head.

Not exciting enough.

Otto gets an idea.

Let's go to the forest to find something exciting for your story!

blows in through the window.

Today they are NOT staying home and napping.
They're going out exploring for exciting things!

Fern makes a quick change
to the story and then the two
friends are off.

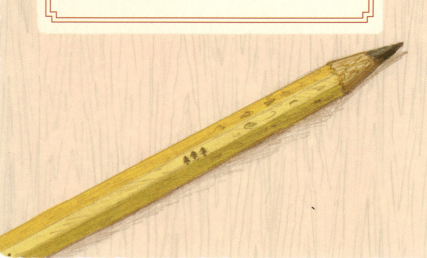

Oh, look—a crowd has gathered.

How delightful, Otto! A race is about to start!

A tortoise is racing a bunny? That doesn't seem very fun to me. Let's keep walking.

TEAM HARE

TEAM Tortoise

SLOW and STEADY

TORTOISE WE BELIEVE IN YOU!

Deeper in the forest is a lovely cottage with a little girl inside. It looks like she's eating something. Shall we see what it is?

Mmmmmmm! Yum!

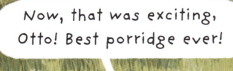

Now, that was exciting, Otto! Best porridge ever!

And what a lovely home.

Porridge isn't going to spice up our story, Fern.

And why were there so many bear things in that house?

What a busy forest! Look at all these creatures.

Was that the same bunny from the race asleep under a tree?
A dish running with a spoon! How strange!
That poor little chicken! Hit on her noggin!
Let's keep going, Fern. No one writes stories about spoons or acorns falling from the sky.
THAT WAY
THIS WAY
WOOL

Oh dear! Fern and Otto better be careful. That wolf looks like trouble.
Why, hello there, my fellow furry friends! Would you like to come with me to Grandma's house? I promise a *big* feast!
No, thank you. We really must be going.

Phew, that was close. A few steps farther, they run into a little girl. She looks very friendly.

Wow, a giant shoe house! I'd love to see what it looks like inside.
I wouldn't want to see what it smells like, Fern!
Look, Otto! That frog is wearing a crown. He must be really important! Maybe we should stop and—
No, it's getting late, Fern. We need to walk fast if we're going to find something perfect for our story.

Here we have three brothers you may know, arguing about building houses. Fern finds their discussion fascinating. But do you think Otto wants to stop and listen?

FINISH
They have some good ideas, Otto. A glass house would be great for naps in the sun.
I think our house is better, Fern.

Speaking of our house, Otto, can we head home? We've been walking for hours, and it's really late. I do have a lot of new ideas for my story.
NO, Fern! We need excitement!
We need . . .

Oh, no!

Hello, dearies! You look scrumptious! Did I hear you say that you're looking for something exciting for a story? I'm writing a story, too. Would you like to be in my story?

Fern and Otto have read enough books to know that they do not *ever* want to be in a witch's story.

Look how fast the friends are moving through the forest now.

You know what would be nice, Fern?

What's that?

To be at home right now, eating a warm supper together. And then you'd sing that song I love while I play the piano.

That does sound nice, Otto.

Oh, thank goodness. Our friends are back home, safe and sound.

Was that exciting enough for you, Otto?

A little *too* exciting for me, Fern.

You know, Fern, I really would love a story about two friends who live in a cozy house on a hill, far away from wolves and witches.

The excitement of the day is too much for Otto. He goes to sleep right after supper. But look at Fern! She has a new idea for a story and gets right to work.

She thinks and writes.
She draws and erases.

She moves some pages
around and throws some out.

She takes a cookie break.

She does a little dance
when a page comes out
particularly well.

She writes some more
and draws some more.
She works hard.

Otto is my best friend.

①

One day, we went on a grand adventure.

②

We were looking for unicorns, genies, and friendly dragons.

③

But it was not the best day. The best days are spent...

⑦

having backyard picnics,

⑧

blowing bubbles,

⑨

But instead we found:
A dish running with a spoon,
and a house made out of a shoe!

④

A big scary
wolf,

a girl dressed
all in red,

⑤

and a WITCH in a house
made of gingerbread.

It was an exciting day.

⑥

flying kites,

⑩

and playing hide-and-
seek with my best
friend, Otto.

⑪

Nothing is more exciting
than having a friend
like that.

Fern pastes and sews the pages together to make a book. She is so proud that her book for Otto is finally complete.

And Otto? Well, he thinks the book is just exciting enough.